written by
janet s. wong

illustrated by
stacey schuett

Alex AND THE Wednesday Chess Club

MARGARET K. MCELDERRY BOOKS   New York   London   Toronto   Sydney

1 Lunchtime Chess

Alex learned chess when he was four.
His parents taught him the rules:
how the pieces move,
how the pieces don't move,
and when to say "Check."

Alex's favorite phrase was "Checkmate, sir!,"
which he liked to shout
as the knight galloped across the board,
jumping over pawns
and knocking the king back—*whack!*—
on his big, round, rolling rump.

Sometimes
at lunchtime
Alex's mother made a special chessboard
out of squares of white and brown bread.

They used olives for pawns.
They used pretzel sticks for bishops.
They cut cheese in L shapes for knights.
Cookies became rooks.
Chocolates became queens.

Alex had long talks with the banana king
about staying in the back corner
to keep from getting smashed to a pulp.

Most of the time he listened.

Alex let the pieces tell him where to move.
Pick me!
  He went first last time!
    Move it, soldier! Coming through!

Trying to decide where to go
and what to do
was the hardest part,
with so many voices interrupting.

Most of the time
Alex worked at getting his pawns
over to the other side of the board
so he could turn them into queens.

He got so very good at turning pawns into queens
that often he had no choice
but to eat a dozen chocolates
at cleanup time.

Alex liked chess.
He was hungry to win.

Of course, he didn't always win.
Sometimes he lost so badly
it made him sick to his stomach.

But most of the time—
win or lose—he loved the way chess left
a sweet taste in his mouth.

Alex loved chess . . .

so who knows why his mother
made him play his next-door neighbor's
moldy old Uncle Hooya.

If Alex was hungry to win,
Uncle Hooya was starving.

He looked ready to bite
somebody's head off.

And he did.

He gobbled Alex's rooks.
He crumbled his bishops.
He swallowed his pawns whole.

Burp!
Alex did not want to play chess ever again.

2 Alex Does NOT Want to Play Chess Ever Again (Really)

But sometimes your mind feels mushy—
you know?

5 + 3 = 6

All mixed up,
and you forget the easy stuff
like how to brush your teeth
or how to tie your shoe.
You do silly things you never thought of doing before.

You clean your closet for no good reason.
Skate backward—
down the stairs.
Eat a third helping of squash.

You join the chess club.

Second week of kindergarten—
Alex's mom asked if he wanted to play chess
with the Wednesday chess club after school.

"You want to join the Wednesday chess club?"
        "No."
"They say it helps with math—"
        "No."
"Andrew and Nicholas think it's fun—"
        "No."

Chess was so—*ummm*—boring, so dry.
Instead Alex chose to learn to swim the butterfly.

His mom asked again in first grade.
    "No."
His mom asked again in second grade.
    "No."
In third grade Alex's mom gave up.

So Alex spent Mondays at the swimming pool
and took piano lessons on Tuesdays and Thursdays
and had football practice on Wednesdays and Fridays
and spent Saturday mornings at games.

Sundays—
well, Sundays were really busy.

Alex forgot about chess . . .

until the day he got an elbow in his eye
and mud in his mouth
and a bruise as big as a football—
all in the first fifteen minutes of the game.

I hate the taste of mud, Alex thought.
He decided to join the chess club.

3 The Wednesday Chess Club

The day of his first chess club meeting,
Alex poked his head through the library door
and took a look inside.

Andrew S. and Andrew H. and Nicholas and Max
and Dylan and Elena were solving chess puzzles.

I can't do this, Alex thought.

Then Alex heard a growl and a yelp
and took another look inside.

Olaf and Fred were in the corner.
Olaf had a headlock on Fred.
Olaf was stuffing Fred's face with cheese puffs.

I can do this, Alex decided,
and he walked into the room.

Coach B. was busy
writing on the board.

COACH B's TOP 10 CHESS TIPS

1. PLAY AT SCHOOL!
2. PLAY AT HOME!
3. PLAY ON THE COMPUTER!
4. PLAY IN TOURNAMENTS!
5. PLAY YOUR GOOD FRIENDS!
6. PLAY YOUR NOT-SO-GOOD FRIENDS!
7. PLAY YOUR PARENTS!
8. PLAY YOUR SISTERS AND BROTHERS!
9. PLAY YOUR COUSINS AND AUNTS AND UNCLES!
10. BUT DON'T PLAY MOLDY OLD UNCLE HOOYA!

4 Alex Becomes Grandmaster of the Chess Excuse

Alex did everything Coach B. told him to do.

He played his family.
He played his friends.
He played his computer.

And he stayed away
from moldy old Uncle Hooya's
greedy, pawn-grabbing fingers.

Alex became a chess maniac
except when there was something good on TV,
or when his friends came over to play video games,
or when he felt like wrestling the dog,
or when he was hungry for macaroni and cheese.

Alex became a chess maniac
when it was time for folding laundry,
or when he had to do his homework,
or when his mother asked him to pick up Potsy's poop,
or when the kitchen smelled like onion pie.

Alex became a chess maniac,
a grandmaster in the making—
Grandmaster of the Chess Excuse.

"Alex, I want you to—"
        "Mom, I'm playing chess on the computer—"
"Well—all right, then I guess I'll do it myself."

The chess excuse worked every time.

GOOD BOOKS

5 Play and Play Some More

Coach B. believes the best way to learn chess
is to play
and do chess puzzles . . .

and play
and play some more.

So every Wednesday
the chess club kids did chess puzzles
and played and played and played.

The last day of Session One—
after seven weeks of play—
they even had their own tournament.

Alex played Andrew S.,
and lost.

Alex played Max,
and lost.

Alex played Nicholas,
and lost.

Alex played the other Andrew,
and lost.

Alex played Dylan,
and lost.

Alex played Elena,
and lost in three minutes flat.

But when Alex played Olaf,
the game ended in a draw.

And when Alex played Fred,
he won a handful of cheese puffs.

And so, at the end of Week Seven
of the Wednesday chess club—
after 140 chess puzzles,
after 630 minutes of games—
everyone was ready
to sign up for the Saturday City Tournament.

Even Fred.
"Can I bring my cheese puffs?" Fred asked.
"If you bring enough for everyone," Coach B. said.

6 Saturday at the City Tournament

On Saturday at the City Tournament
Fred brought enough cheese puffs for everyone.
Everyone.

Tournament chess
is not just about chess.

It's about
sharing cheese puffs,
when to go to the bathroom,
what to do when the person on the other side
is making you nervous,
and how much money to spend
on soda pop and candy.

It's about
how fast or how slow to play,
playing football outside between games,
and telling your parents all about your smart moves
so they'll give you more money
for soda pop and candy.

The best part about tournament chess
is winning,
of course—

and the worst part about tournament chess
is sitting there for twenty minutes,
waiting for the other guy to make a move . . .
and when he finally does move,
you don't see
he's going to smash you
up the middle . . .

and you do the first thing that pops into your mind,
which is really, really dumb,
but you really, really, really have to pee,
and that's all you can think about for heaven's sake,
and—*zap! bang!*—you've been whooped . . .

and he shakes your sweaty hand and smiles
until—*ick!*—all of a sudden he realizes

you've been eating Fred's cheese puffs.

Game One:
Board 43

Alex is unrated.
His opponent, Owen Option-Checker, is rated 790.
Alex loses this very long game,
which is kind of close—

almost—

in the beginning,
for a move or two, at least.

The most important thing is
Alex makes it to the
bathroom in time.

Game Two:
Board 51

Alex plays Miss Lightning-Quick,
who is also unrated
but is some kind of kindergarten genius
with a mind like a minicomputer.
Alex knows
he can make Miss Lightning-Quick crazy
by playing slow,

so in between his moves
he counts
the number of squares
on the board,
on the ceiling,
and on the floor.

A waste of time for nothing,
as Miss Lightning-Quick is playing five moves ahead
and knows what Alex is going to do
before he does.

When Alex sees the pizza delivery man
pass by the gym doors,
he forfeits.

But all is not lost,
as Alex is first
in line
for pizza.

Game Three:
Board 69 (the second-to-last board)

The best thing is
Fred is on Board 70,
passing cheese puffs under the table,
while Alex's opponent is turning blue
from too much soda pop and candy—

and Alex wins
just before Little Boy Blue-in-the-Face loses
his lunch.

Game Four:
Board 53

The kid's name is George,
and he is so nice
I hate to beat him—

but—

"Good game, George. Better luck next time!"
        "Great game, Alex! You're really good!
        Hey, you want to go outside and play some football?"

8 The Return of Hooya

Game Five:
Board 49

Alex has a rating!
580 is not exactly the kind of rating he wanted,
but it could be worse.

It could be worse—
he could be playing the state champion's
surly baby brother,

his next-door neighbor's Little Cousin Hooya!

Oh—
and he is.

Uncle Hooya walks Little Hooya to his seat.
"Look, it is Alex," Uncle Hooya says to Little Hooya,
showing his hungry teeth.

Uncle Hooya knocks Little Hooya on the head.
"This time, no excuses! This time, win!"

Little Hooya opens with a regular, boring pawn move.
Alex scraps his regular, boring pawn move
for something different,
something risky,
something daring—

he brings out the knight.

Little Hooya brings out a pawn.

Alex brings out the other knight.

Little Hooya takes him.

Alex thinks, *How did I miss that?*
Alex takes Little Hooya's pawn.
A pawn for a knight—pitiful. Alex bites his lip.

It's a bloody battlefield out there
with a new prisoner every five seconds.

And Alex is losing.
Fast.

Little Hooya is drooling.

Alex is down to his king, a rook, a knight, and a pawn,
playing on the run.
Alex's rook is screaming at him,
Attack!

  No, Little Hooya won't fall for that, he tells his rook.
Try it—be brave, Alex! the rook calls out.

So Alex puts the rook in position,
attacking Little Hooya's bishop
while Little Hooya is looking at the trophies.

"Your move," Alex says,
and Little Hooya turns around.
Somehow he doesn't see the rook attack!
He moves the wrong piece.
Whack!

This is fun! Alex thinks,
and he sinks low into his chair
so he can listen a little more carefully
to his very brave and clever rook.

Little Hooya is so mad at himself for losing another piece
that his ears are turning red.

Now the pawn is talking to Alex.
Promote me! he is shouting.

And all of a sudden Alex remembers
olives turning into chocolates—
mmmmmmm—

and
square
by
square
by
square
his
pawn
creeps
closer
and
closer
and
closer
until—

yes!—

Alex does it!

Little Hooya takes Alex's pawn
and tosses Alex's lost queen
back on the board.

Little Hooya's eyes are full of panic,
darting around the room,
searching for Uncle Hooya.

Alex sets up another trap.
His queen is whispering something strange.
He moves her out into the open.

Little Hooya's eyes widen
as he sees Alex's queen, unguarded.
Little Hooya's knight rushes toward her,
whisking her away
and leaving Little Hooya's king wide open—

and with one easy move
Alex's rook has Little Hooya's king trapped!

CheckMATE!
Alex wins!

Alex's Top 10 Chess Tips

1. Get out in the center. You can win a million different ways, but your chances are best if you get control of the center of the board.

2. Don't trade for junk. Just because you *can* take a piece doesn't mean you have to take it.

3. Castle early in the game. With the castle you get to move the rook and the king at the same time—so why wouldn't you want to do it?

4. Use pawns to defend. Hooray for pawns! A wall of pawns makes a great defense. Or march them to the other side and promote them.

5. Set your table with a fork. With a fork you aim at two pieces at the same time, so you'll capture at least one of them.

6. Watch for attacks. Before you move always make sure your pieces are safe! Attacking pieces can sit out in the open or hide behind other pieces.

7. Fill the holes. Don't go where there's a crowd. Look for holes—safe, open squares in a good spot!

8. Think ahead. It's fun to play fast, but most of the time slow play is better because it gives you time to think ahead. Some people like to sit on their hands to keep from moving too quickly.

9. Keep track of your moves. Sometimes I forget (just for a second) whose move it is—and then if it's a dirty, rotten rat on the other side, he'll try to take two turns in a row! Our coach makes us practice recording the moves—on paper and in our minds.

10. Play! And don't worry about those Hooyas!

To the players and coaches
of the St. Thomas School Chess Team
—J. W.

To Floy, with love
—S. S.

Margaret K. McElderry Books • An imprint of Simon & Schuster Children's Publishing Division • 1230 Avenue of the Americas
New York, New York 10020 • Text copyright © 2004 by Janet S. Wong • Illustrations copyright © 2004 by Stacey Schuett
All rights reserved, including the right of reproduction in whole or in part in any form. • Book design by Sonia Chaghatzbanian
The text for this book is set in Adobe Caslon. • The illustrations are rendered in gouache and ink on Arches watercolor paper.
Manufactured in China • 2 4 6 8 10 9 7 5 3 1 • Library of Congress Cataloging-in-Publication Data • Wong, Janet S.
Alex and the Wednesday chess club / Janet S. Wong ; illustrated by Stacey Schuett.—1st ed. • p. cm.
Summary: Alex quits playing chess after losing a game to Uncle Hooya; but when other activities fail to satisfy him, he gives his favorite
game another try by joining the chess club. • ISBN 0-689-85890-6 (hardcover) • [1. Chess—Fiction. 2. Winning and losing—Fiction.]
I. Schuett, Stacey, ill. II. Title. • PZ7.W842115Al 2004 • [Fic]—dc21 • 2003009586

FIRST
EDITION